Tails of Spring Break

Tails of Spring Break

Anne Warren Smith

Albert Whitman & Company
Chicago, Illinois

Also by Anne Warren Smith:
Turkey Monster Thanksgiving
Bittersweet Summer

Library of Congress Cataloging-in-Publication data
Smith, Anne Warren.
Tails of spring break/by Anne Warren Smith
p. cm.
Summary: Katie endures a challenging spring break during which she is
forced to share her bedroom with Claire, her difficult neighbor and
classmate, and run a pet-sitting business at the same time.
ISBN 978-0-8075-6358-8 (hardcover)
ISBN 978-0-8075-6359-5 (paperback)
[1. Pet-sitting—Fiction. 2. Interpersonal relations—Fiction.
3. Neighbors—Fiction 4. Spring break—Fiction.] I. Title.
PZ7.S6427Tai 2005   [Fic]—dc22   2004021642

10 9 8 7 6 5 4 3 2 LB 16 15 14 13 12

Designed by Lindaanne Donohoe

For more information about Albert Whitman & Company,
visit our website at www.albertwhitman.com.

For Amity,
who brought us the original "Muffin."

Contents

1 My Great Idea 1

2 The Cat Moves In 8

3 Terrible News 14

4 Claire Plummer Moves In 20

5 No Tarantulas, Please! 26

6 Mom Calls to Chat 32

7 Talking to Mothers 37

8 China Speaks Up 44

9 Too Many Worries 50

10 Claire Writes Things Down 57

11 Fish, Fish, and More Fish 61

12 Where is China Cat? 68

13 China is Everywhere 75

14 Tyler Speaks Up 78

15 Claire "Fixes" Things 82

16 Disaster! 87

17 More Trouble 93

18 "You Were a Good Swimmer" . . . 97

19 Facing Mrs. Anderson 104

20 China—Still Wild 109

21 Tea with Ruby 113

22 Two Moms 108

23 The Final Tail 125

Contents

1. My Great Idea 1
2. The Cat Rolls In 8
3. Technicians 14
4. Can Chocolate Move In 21
5. Neither Are Bleats 30
6. Are More Cats to Come . . . . .
7. Farina to Mothers 37
8. Cattle Speaks Up 41
9. The Next World 50
10. Chloe Writes Things Down . . . 57
11. Tush, Plan, and More Fish . . . 61
12. Where Is Chloe Now 65
13. Chloe Is Everywhere 73
14. The Sea Is Up 75
15. Chloe Does Things 82
16. It Began 87
17. Mars Is Far 94
18. You Were a Good Engineer . . . 99
19. Retha Gets Anderson 104
20. A Most Sad World 120
21. Jane Is a Gathering . . . . . .
     Foot . . . .
22. The First Day 139

Chapter 1

My Great Idea

On the last day of school before spring vacation, it sounded like almost every kid in my fourth grade class was getting away from Oregon. They were going places where the sun was shining. Places like Disneyland and San Diego. Even Hawaii!

Just before recess, Ms. Morgan, my most favorite teacher ever, made a huge mistake. "Surely a few of you will stay in town for vacation, and that's nice, too," she said. "Who's staying here? Let's see your hands."

I raised my hand and looked around. I might have known. My hand was the only one.

"Anyone else?" Ms. Morgan asked, looking sorry she'd brought it up. "Anyone besides Katie?"

No one moved.

I thunked my forehead down on my desk. Just then, the recess bell rang.

My best friend, Sierra, patted my shoulder. "Too bad you raised your hand," she said.

"My Country 'Tis of Thee," someone sang. In perfect pitch. Of course, it was Claire Plummer. She'd been PERFECT AT EVERYTHING since second grade. She'd been singing patriotic songs a hundred times a day. She and her dad were going to Washington, D.C. for spring vacation. She'd told everyone she expected to meet the President.

I leaped up and grabbed Sierra's arm. "Let me out of here." We rushed across the room, away from Claire and her song. "I'm sick to death of hearing about Washington, D.C.," I leaned on the window sill and stared out at a wet school-yard. Cars moved past, their lights on, their wipers going. A lone biker pedaled hunched over, dressed from head to toe in yellow rain gear.

Claire was right behind us. "Our nation's capital is on the east coast," she said. "Want to see it on the globe?"

"Sierra's going to Hawaii," I said. "Nicer than what you're doing."

"The worst is what you're doing," Claire said. "Staying in rainy old Oregon."

"Excuse us," I said. Sierra and I pushed past Claire and went out to the water fountain in the hall.

"No wonder nobody likes Claire Plummer," Sierra said. "Maybe someday, she'll move to a house that isn't across the street from you."

"Maybe someday, my dad won't make me walk to school with her." I held the lever down and let Sierra drink. "He thinks it's safer to walk in pairs." He also thought Claire and I had stuff in common because we didn't have mothers at home. Claire's mom had died when we were in second grade. Mine had already left home by then because she wanted to be a famous Country and Western singer.

"I wish you could come with us to Hawaii." Sierra wiped water from her chin with the cuff of her red blouse. "It would be loads more fun."

"I'll be stuck here," I said. "Rusting."

"Mom almost decided not to go," Sierra said. "We're so worried about China Cat."

"I thought there was a cat motel," I said.

"There is." Sierra jammed her hands into her jumper pockets. "Motel La Paws. They don't really want her. They said she yowled last year. The whole time."

"Poor China," I said. "She didn't know anybody at Motel La Paws. She was lonely."

"Mom told them she doesn't yowl anymore," Sierra said. "So they said okay. But we know she's going to hate it."

I thought about China's soft fur, mostly yellow, with white streaks. I loved the way she twitched her ears and tipped her head when you talked to her. "Wow!" I said. "I'm getting a great idea."

Sierra held up both hands. "No, Katie. Please. No great ideas."

I tugged Sierra down the hall. "We have to use the phone in the office, right now."

Sierra shook her arm away. "Sometimes, your great ideas turn out bad."

"You'll like this one," I said. "You don't need a cat motel. China can stay at *my* house while you're gone." I skipped ahead of Sierra. Maybe this vacation would be fun, after all. "At my house," I said, "she won't be lonely. China loves me. She lets me pat her from her nose to the tip of her tail."

"Hold it." Sierra skidded to a stop. "You know how to pat her, but you don't know how to take care of her."

"I've had pets." I pulled on Sierra's hand. "Remember my inchworm?"

"It dried up," Sierra said.

"Not right away," I said. "Come on."

She shook her head and followed me into the office.

"Sierra has to call her mother, please," I told Betty, the secretary. "It's about spring break."

Sierra put her hands behind her back.

5

"Haven't we been best friends forever?"
I asked. "Since day care?"

She nodded slowly.

"Every time I come to your house," I said,
"China rubs against me and purrs."

"She does like you," Sierra said. She pulled
the phone toward her and dialed.

By the time she hung up, she was smiling.
"Mom thinks you can do it," she said. "She's calling
your dad to make sure. She said she'd pay you."

"Pay me?"

"Five dollars a day. For being a pet sitter."

"Oh my gosh," I said. "Really? Like a real job?"
I danced out of the office and down the hall. "I'll
be a great pet sitter," I called back to Sierra. "This
is the beginning of something big."

Sierra ran after me. "Slow down," she said.

"The world is full of lonely animals," I told her,
"especially at vacation time when their people
go away. I'll start with cats and move on to dogs.
Horses. Canaries. Lions and tigers."

Sierra shook her head. "You are out of
control."

"I'm going to be the most wonderful pet sitter," I said. "Someday, you'll see my commercials on TV." I waved an imaginary sign over my head. What would it say?

CALL KATIE JORDAN
YOUR LONELY PET'S BEST FRIEND

Chapter 2

The Cat Moves In

When I got home from school, my four-year-old brother met me at the door. "Yippee," Tyler yelled. "We get to have a cat." He bounced away on his kangaroo ball, his red hair flopping up and down as he went. "Yippee! Yippee!"

"Cats are sensitive animals," I said. "You can't be yelling like that around China Cat."

He bounced back to me. "Can I play with her?" he asked. He made his voice a tiny bit softer.

"Most of the time, I'll be playing with her," I told him. "They're going to pay me. It's a real job."

Dad came down the hall from the room that was his home office. "I told Sierra's mother we could do it," he said. "But then, I got sort of worried. Is it a nice cat?"

"China lets you rub her tummy," I said. "You're going to love her."

"Yippee!" Tyler shouted. And then, he clapped his hand over his mouth. "Yippee," he whispered through his hand. "I can be very quiet."

Dad grinned and tucked Tyler's tee shirt into his corduroys. "That'll be a nice change," he said.

A while later, Sierra and her family came to the door. Under their rain jackets, they were dressed for Hawaii in shorts and tee shirts.

"Thanks for doing this, Katie," Mrs. Dymond said. She cuddled China in her arms. China stretched and purred.

"All right!" Tyler yelled. "A BIG cat – super!"

China's eyes got round. She stared at Tyler.

"Oh, oh," Tyler said. "Whisper."

"We brought everything she needs," Mrs. Dymond said. "Her litter box— she never goes outside, you know. And her food and her bed."

Mr. Dymond came in carrying China's wicker bed. He set it down and fluffed China's soft, green pillows.

China Cat looked at her bed. Her eyes grew bigger. Her tail stiffened. All at once, she hissed. With one fast strike, she raked her claws across Mrs. Dymond's hand. Mrs. Dymond shrieked.

China landed on the floor. Her fur formed jagged spikes along her humped back. She looked like a yellow Halloween cat.

I grabbed Sierra's hand.

China sniffed at the front door. Then she turned and stalked down the hall, her tail stiff and angry.

Mrs. Dymond dabbed at her hand with a tissue. "She knows we're leaving her. She's very upset."

Sierra ran with me down the hall just as China swished into Tyler's room and under his bed. We lay on our stomachs and stared. Two yellow slitted eyes stared back. China growled.

"I didn't know cats growled," I said. "That's creepy."

"She only growls when she hates something," Sierra said. "Maybe she heard about your inch-worm."

I gulped.

"We have to leave," Mr. Dymond called. "Airplanes don't wait."

Sierra started to cry. "My poor kitty," she wailed.

"NOW," Mr. Dymond called.

Sierra stood up and rubbed her hands against her red cheeks.

"I'll play with her," I told her. "I'll make her stop feeling lonely."

Sierra shook her head. "I don't know if you can." She ran down the hall.

"You'll see," I said as I ran after her. "It'll be okay. I promise."

Sierra and her mother scooted out the door. Sierra looked back at me just before she got into the car. "Try as hard as you can," she called.

After they drove away, I closed the door and sagged against it. I looked at Dad and Tyler. "She's usually sweet," I said. "I've never seen her like this. Never."

They stared at me. Dad shook his head.

We went down the hall to Tyler's room, knelt down, and looked under his bed.

"Why is she there?" Tyler asked. "I keep stuff under my bed."

"I see," Dad said. "What a mess." He piled little racecars against the wall and leaned forward. "Hi, China," he said. He held his hand out.

"Hiss," China said.

Dad pulled his hand back. He stood up.

"Maybe food will help," I said.

Dad brought a bowl of cat food to Tyler's room. When he slid it under the bed, China glared at him. She hissed again.

"Now, it smells in here," Tyler said. He held his nose. "My room smells like a fish."

"Your room always smells like something," I told him.

"Eat your nice dinner," Tyler said. China didn't move. Her slitted eyes didn't change.

"I need to get back to work," Dad said. His voice sounded worried again. He went down the hall to his office.

"This cat isn't any fun," Tyler said after a while. He frowned at me.

"How am I going to make her feel better," I asked, "if she won't come out?"

Tyler sat up. "Are they really going to pay you money?"

I nodded. "I'm going to buy an artist's box. I saw one at the store. It has pastels, and watercolors, and beautiful gel pens."

I had figured I'd share my artist's box with Sierra. I shivered. If taking care of China didn't work out, Sierra might stop being my friend.

Chapter 3

Terrible News

Saturday morning at breakfast, Tyler mashed his cereal into brown mush. "I'm tired." He yawned and put his head on the table next to his dish.

"Me, too," Dad said. He blinked at the front page of the newspaper. "In the middle of the night, a little boy climbed into bed with me."

"The cat did those noises," Tyler said, "all night long. Like this." He growled a low creepy sound. "Grrrrrr."

"Pretty good," Dad said. "You almost sound like her."

"China's getting used to us," I said. "I know this cat. Pretty soon she'll be purring around, asking us to pat her."

"I thought this was going to be the perfect vacation," Dad said. "Quiet and relaxing." He got up to clear the table. "I thought we'd sleep late and enjoy not being on a schedule."

"I'll be very busy with my new business," I said.

Dad wasn't listening. He poured more coffee and wandered down the hall.

As soon as he was gone, I covered the family room table with markers and colored paper. China had shown me how upset a pet could be. All over town, pets were watching their owners pack suitcases. Those pets needed help. They needed me!

Tyler went past with the big flashlight, snapping it on and off. "She has whiskers coming out of her eyebrows," he yelled a few minutes later.

"Don't be loud," I called. "This is her adjustment time."

"I'm just looking at her," Tyler said.

I held up a flyer. Cute puppies played around the edges of this one. All the flyers said the same thing:

GOING AWAY?

CALL KATIE JORDAN

I'LL BE YOUR LONELY PET'S BEST FRIEND

CHEAP. NO SNAKES. 708-7755

The pet owners didn't know yet about my business. I had to get the word out. The drizzle outside had turned into a downpour, but I'd go anyway. I put on my jacket and tucked the flyers under the front of it. "Back in a minute," I called.

I splashed around the block and dropped a flyer on every porch.

When I got back to my own house, Mr. Plummer, Claire's dad, was running down my porch steps. He nodded to me as he pushed up his big black umbrella and ran across the street to his own house.

As soon as I stepped inside, Dad rushed past me with a pile of my dirty clothes in his arms.

"Pick up those blocks," he told Tyler.

"Where are you taking my clothes?" I asked.

Dad disappeared into the utility room and came back empty-handed. "Claire Plummer has to stay with us this week," he said. "Her grandpa is very sick. Her dad has to go to Chicago to be with him."

"But they're going to Washington, D.C.," I said.

"Not anymore," Dad said. "She'll be sleeping in the other bed in your room."

"No way," I yelled. "No way is Claire Plummer going to stay here!"

Dad frowned at me. "We need to talk about your attitude," he said. "When neighbors need help, we say yes." He picked up shoes and papers from the family room floor and rushed down the hall to my room.

I followed him. "Can't she sleep in Tyler's room?"

"No." He'd gotten out clean sheets. He flapped one onto the spare bed and tucked it in.

"On the couch?"

"No." He finished with the spare bed and then looked at my bed. In a minute he had it straight and tidy. "Why is your jacket so wet?" he asked. "Hang it in the utility room. And do something about your closet. The doors don't close."

"I like them that way."

"Dresser drawers, too," Dad said.

I stomped down the hall and tossed my jacket onto the dryer. I ran back to my room. "Hold everything," I yelled. "She can't see Mom!" I pointed to the life-sized poster of Mom beside the dresser. Dad turned to look.

Mom was wearing white cowboy boots, a cute short white skirt, and a red vest that sparkled. She was playing her guitar, but it was *me* she was looking at. *Me*, she was smiling at. Even though she and Dad had been divorced for three years. Even though she'd changed her name to Roxanne Winter and had gotten famous.

"I don't want to share Mom with Claire," I said. "Claire is mean."

Dad's face softened. He sat down on my bed and held out his arms. "I know you sometimes don't get along."

I climbed up beside him. "Nobody gets along with Claire." I blinked back tears and burrowed my head into his shirt. He smelled of books and coffee.

"I want you to be nice to her," he said. "It'll be good practice."

"Practice? For what?"

"Living a good life." He gave me a squeeze.

"That doesn't make sense." I wiggled off his lap. "Help me take Mom down."

We peeled the tape loose and rolled up the poster. Dad ran the vacuum cleaner while I scooped up things just before he got to them. I shoved everything into my closet and forced the doors closed. I slid the rolled-up poster of Mom under my bed. "It's only for a week," I whispered to her. I stopped to think. "A very long week."

Chapter 4

Claire Plummer Moves In

That afternoon, Claire carried in a mountain of blue suitcases and matching tote bags. We stacked them in front of my closet doors. "You'll sleep in that bed," I said. I plopped down on my own bed.

Down the hall, China was still making those creepy growls. Tyler was supposed to be napping, but I could hear him on Dad's bed, singing a day-care song about ducks.

Claire sat across from me on the other bed and twirled a blonde curl around her finger. "I wanted to go help take care of my grandpa," she said, finally letting her curl rest. "But my father said no."

"That's too bad your grandpa got sick." I unlaced my sneakers and kicked them off. "And you're missing Washington, D.C."

"I never thought I'd be at *your* house for spring break," she said. She sighed.

In the next room, Dad cleared his throat and wadded up some papers. "Be nice to her," he'd said. Talk about impossible.

"You sure brought a lot of stuff," I said.

"I should unpack." Claire slid off the bed and opened a tote bag. She unrolled a small rug, light blue, and put it on the floor between our beds. She set a blue ruffled pillow on her bed and a blue clock radio next to my lamp. She laid blue-and-white striped pajamas at the foot of the bed. She set out a white teddy bear. It had a sweater on, baby blue. None of her stuff went with my orange-and-white polka-dot spreads.

She turned to me. "I have to hang up some things," she said.

"In the closet?"

She looked down her nose. "Of course, in the closet. On hangers. That's how we keep clothes nice."

"Here goes," I said. I forced the closet doors open and shoved all my stuff to one side. We jammed in Claire's dresses and skirts and tops. "What did you bring all those for?" I asked. "We'll just be wearing jeans this week."

"I like to look nicer than that," Claire said. She unzipped her fashion boots and pulled them off. She set them in the corner.

My stomach began to hurt. I went back to sit on my bed.

From another tote bag, Claire pulled out a photo album, a box of pale blue notepaper, pens and pencils, and a package of glittery butterfly stickers. "I'm going to write to all my pen pals this week," she explained. "I have their pictures in this album. Ten of them."

"Nobody has ten pen pals." I watched her

stack up my books so she could put her album on the shelf.

"My favorite one lives in France." She held up a plastic box that rattled. "I'm stringing beads for a bracelet for my Aunt Kirsten," she said. "Want to see?"

I squinted at the little beads. "Don't you ever spill them?"

"Never." Claire set the box of beads on her album. "I hope Tyler won't come in here." She shuddered and made a face. "Where is he, anyway?"

"He's sort of taking a nap in Dad's room. Sierra's cat is under his bed."

Claire raised her eyebrows. "Sierra's cat?"

"I take care of lonely pets now. It's my new business. People are paying me."

Claire pushed empty tote bags and suitcases under her bed. Lucky thing Dad had vacuumed under there.

"Are you organized enough to have a business?" she asked.

"I'm very organized."

Claire shook her head. "I remember that Thanksgiving dinner you planned. A disaster!"

"Ms. Morgan loved my dinner."

"I bet she thought it was weird," Claire said with a frown. "Not one thing was traditional."

She was still mad about our teacher coming to my house instead of hers. I lay back on my bed remembering my decorations and the food I made, and Tyler running away to tame the turkey monster. What a day it had been. I sat back up. "I handed out pet sitter flyers this morning. People will be calling."

"You handed out flyers?" Claire looked up from rearranging my shell collection.

"Be careful of those."

"Don't you ever dust them?" She blew at the shells and wrinkled her nose. "Where are your lists for your business?"

"My business doesn't need lists."

"You're supposed to write things down so you don't forget something important." She left my shells and opened another tote bag and pulled out a notebook. She flipped it open. "I make lists about everything. This page has all my pen pals. This one is all the books I ever read. This is my list of what to pack for Washington, D.C." She looked sad as she turned that page.

I rummaged in my bookshelf until I found my own notebook. "First," I said, "I'll list each pet."

"And their phone numbers."

"That's really stupid, Claire. Pets don't talk on the phone."

"For emergencies, dummy," Claire said. "My father told your father how to reach him. He gave him the number for my doctor too."

Had Sierra's family left any phone numbers? I wasn't sure. China had better not get sick.

Just then, while we were talking about phones, our phone rang. I heard Dad answer it.

In a minute, he came to the door. "That was Mrs. Anderson from next door. I don't know what made her think of it, but she wants you to take care of Muffin this week."

Chapter 5

No Tarantulas, Please!

W e need to go over there," Dad said, "to find out what she wants done. Come with us, Claire."

Claire already had her jacket on.

"Wait a minute," I said.

"I'd better come," Claire said. "You'll forget things. Bring that notebook."

A few minutes later, the four of us crossed the yard to the Andersons' house. "Mrs. Anderson's my friend," Tyler told Claire. "She sometimes takes care of me. She brings her knitting needles."

As Mrs. Anderson let us in, her dog Muffin scooted between our legs and around the room, yapping hello. "Hi there, little dust mop." I squatted down to pat her head as she rushed past me.

Mrs. Anderson grabbed a paper towel and ran after Muffin, pushing the towel across the floor.

"What's she doing?" Claire whispered.

"Wiping up piddle," I answered. "I forgot about that." Claire made a face and went to stand by the door.

"A few excitement drops, the little dear," Mrs. Anderson said, panting a bit. She threw away the paper towel and washed her hands at the kitchen sink. "We're going tomorrow to visit the grandchildren," she told us. "I kept thinking we'd take Muffin, but then I found Katie's clever flyer."

Dad looked confused, but Mrs. Anderson didn't give him time to ask about the flyer.

"I'll want you to feed her once in the morning and once at night. Let her out in the yard after she eats. It would be nice if you could take her for a walk, but she's such a silly girl when it rains.

She hates getting her feet wet. The best thing
is to exercise her in the house. Throw the ball
for her." She looked down at Muffin and smiled.
"The little dear."

"Write all that down," Claire said.

"I was already doing it," I said. I opened my
notebook.

"Here's her towel for wiping her off if she gets
wet," Mrs. Anderson said. "She thinks that's quite
a game, the little rascal." She set the towel next
to Muffin's food.

"And the vet," she continued. She opened
the phone book and looked through the bottoms
of her glasses for the number. "This is just in
case . . ."

"Told you so," Claire whispered.

Mrs. Anderson looked up from the phone
book. "Will Claire be helping you?"

"No," I answered.

"Please bring in the mail," Mrs. Anderson
said. "And the newspaper." She handed me a key
that had a piece of red yarn tied to it. "This will
let you in the kitchen door."

"You have to lock up every time you leave,"
Dad said. "I'll come with you a couple of times,
to get you started."

As we squished through the wet grass on the
way back to our house, my brain buzzed with all
the instructions. Feed Muffin. Let her out. Let her
in. Dry her off. Get the mail. Lock the door. A lot
to remember!

Then I thought about how happy Muffin
would be when I opened her door. I'd brush her
and maybe give her a bath. We'd play a game with
the towel. She'd lick my cheek and crawl into my
arms. No more lonely dog.

As we walked in, the phone rang. Could it be
another customer?

"Hello," Dad said. "You're calling about what?
A tarantula?"

"No, no, no," I whispered, tugging on his
sleeve.

Tyler pulled on Dad's other sleeve. "Great!"
he shouted.

Dad hushed us. "How did you get this number?"
he asked. As he listened, he began to frown. At me!

"May I call you back?" Dad asked. He waved his arm. "Paper," he whispered. "Pencil."

"At my house," Claire said, "we keep paper and pencil next to the phone."

"Be quiet, Claire," I said. I gave Dad my notebook and the pencil. He wrote down a number, hung up the phone, and looked at me. "You made flyers?"

"For advertising my business," I said.

"A tarantula sounds very good," Tyler said to Dad. "Better than a cat."

"What business?" Dad asked.

"I'm already doing it, Dad. I'm taking care of lonely pets. China Cat. And Muffin."

"How many flyers?"

I hated it when Dad's voice barked at me. "Just around our block."

"This man has a tarantula," Dad said. "And I don't know him. The man. I don't know the man *or* the tarantula." He took off his glasses and rubbed his eyes. "You can't be going into houses of people we don't know."

"But . . ." I zipped my jacket zipper up and down.

"That's exactly what my father would have said," Claire told us. She shook her blonde curls and sat down across from Dad at the table. As if it were *her* table!

Dad rubbed at his forehead. "We'll have to call him and tell him no. Maybe that's the only call you'll get."

The phone rang. We stared at it. It rang again.

"You mustn't say 'hello'," I told Dad. "Say, 'Thanks for calling your lonely pet's best friend.'"

Chapter 6

Mom Calls to Chat

D ad frowned at me and picked up the phone. "Hello," he said. Then, "Hi, Roxie."

"It's Mom!" I ran to stand beside him.

Tyler got to talk to her first but, as usual, he hardly said a word. He mostly listened and nodded. "She can't see you nod," I said, and Dad said, "Hush, leave him alone." Then, he handed the phone to me, and it was my turn.

Mom's voice on the phone was like listening to her sing. "We're setting up to do a show," she told me. "Pretty soon they'll ask me to sing into my mike, to make sure the sound is balanced."

"Where are you?" I asked.

"Tulsa, Oklahoma," she said. "Near Texas."

Over the phone, I could hear the guitar and fiddle sounds of her band. Mom's life was so exciting. "Do you have on your red sparkly vest?" I asked.

She laughed. "Actually, tonight it's going to be green sparkles. Tell me what you've been up to."

I told her it was spring break, and everyone else had gone somewhere. But it was okay because I had a business. I'd grown again. I needed some new jeans.

About then, I heard someone call to her. "I'm sorry," she said, "but I have to go now. I'll call you again, Honey."

"Bye, Mom," I said. As I hung up, I wished I'd told her about how I might buy an artist box. As I turned around, I saw Claire.

She was still sitting at the table, but she held her arms across her stomach as if she had a pain. Pink blotches covered her cheeks. She stared at me with a strange look on her face.

"Are you sick?" I asked.

She stood up. "I hate you, Katie Jordan," she said in a tight little voice. "It's not fair. Your mom can *call* you." She ran down the hall into my bedroom and slammed the door.

I started to follow.

"Wait," Dad said. "I think she needs to be alone." He took off his glasses and rubbed his forehead. "Too bad. Too bad."

"What's too bad, Daddy?" Tyler asked.

"Claire can't get phone calls from her mother," he said. "Her mother's dead."

"We're lucky, huh, Daddy," Tyler said. He climbed up onto Dad's lap.

"Pretty lucky," Dad answered. He hugged Tyler close, but he was blinking as if he had something in his eye. Was he blinking back a tear? I couldn't tell.

"Now, what do we do?" I asked. "She's in my bedroom."

Dad stopped blinking and looked hard at me. "You're being kind to lonely pets. Seems like you could be kind to Claire."

As I stared out at the wet bushes in the backyard, I saw Claire's sad face. I should be nicer to her. But then, I remembered all the mean things she said. "I can't, Dad." I lowered my voice. "She's awful." As I shoved my hands into my jacket pockets, my fingers touched the Andersons' house key. "Here," I said, pulling it out. "We need a safe place for this."

Dad's face brightened. "The two of you could . . . ," he began.

"No way!" I yelled. "It's *my* business." I threw the key onto the table.

"You're sharing with me," Tyler said. "It's my bed China's under." He slid off Dad's lap and went down the hall.

"First of all," I said, "everybody but us went somewhere good for spring break." I lowered my voice. "And the worst person in fourth grade is living in my bedroom." I flung myself into a chair. "And China Cat doesn't cuddle and purr, the way I thought she would."

Dad tipped his head to one side. "Listen to that," he said. "Tyler's singing."

I listened as the words to "Three Blind Mice" drifted down the hall.

Dad began to smile. "Tyler knows how to make a lonely cat feel better," he said, "and he's only four years old."

I stopped grinning as I figured out what he meant. Since I was older, he thought I could share everything with Claire. Well, he was wrong. I'd have to be an old lady before that would happen.

"Being nice to a cat is easy," I told him. "Being nice to Claire is impossible." I went down the hall to Tyler's room.

Chapter 7

Talking to Mothers

L ater that afternoon, Claire finally came out of my bedroom. She sat at the table and wrote letters to her pen pals. Still later, she helped Dad and me fix supper. None of us mentioned Mom's phone call. Claire reminded us to use place mats and napkins. And forks, as if we would have eaten macaroni and cheese with our fingers. "We should have a centerpiece," she said.

"We do centerpieces on holidays," I told her.

"Where's Tyler?" Dad asked. "Still in there with China?"

"Whatever he's doing is working," I said. "She's not growling."

Dad handed the paper napkins to Claire, who set them around the table. "We want you to feel at home with us, Claire," he said. "What would help you feel comfortable?"

She sat down at the table, thinking. "I should have brought some games. We could play games."

"We have tons of games," I told her. From the kitchen, Dad sent me a thumbs-up.

I frowned at him. Playing games with Claire was not my idea of fun. I sighed. Then I remembered her sad face. I would try to cheer her up.

After dinner, Tyler built things with Legos in his room and talked to China who was growling again. Dad turned on the TV to a basketball game.

When Claire and I opened the game cupboard, things began to slide out. "I might have known," she said. "Everything in your game cupboard is mixed up."

First, she made us find the Sorry pieces and

put them in their box. Then, the checkers. Then, the Chutes and Ladders. Then, the worst thing— the cards. "I might have known," she said again as she separated the decks.

I slapped a deck of cards onto the floor. "That's it," I said. "Play by yourself."

She looked surprised.

"I'm going to read to China. I *do* have a business." I stepped over all the cards and went to find my book.

"Big deal," Claire said. I heard her ask Dad to play Concentration, and I couldn't believe it when he said yes. As I lay on Tyler's bed and read my book out loud, I could hear them in the family room, laughing and having a great time. Claire even beat Dad. They came down the hall to tell me.

I turned my back on them. China growled just then, and I was glad.

Later when Claire and I got ready for bed, she kept getting in the way. "Excuse me," I said, as I searched for my pajamas that were lost because of cleaning up my room.

"Excuse *me*," she said as she pushed past me with her toothbrush in her hand.

"Excuse ME," I said when we both ended up at the sink.

"Excuse ME," she said and turned off the bathroom light before I was done.

I flopped on my bed while Claire rubbed something smelly into her hair and started brushing it. "You're dropping yellow hair all over my room," I said.

"Your hair would look nicer if you brushed it now and then." She held up a blue-and-white plastic mirror and smiled into it.

I stared at the empty space on the wall where my poster used to hang. Most nights, I pretended Mom and I were having a talk before I went to sleep. Now, because of Claire, I couldn't even do that. I wondered if Mom was singing right that minute. In Tulsa, Oklahoma.

Claire fluffed her hair and set the brush in her lap. "What does she say when she calls?" she asked.

How could she know I'd been thinking about

Mom? I twisted my sheet into a flower in my hand and pushed my face into it. "Not much," I said into the flower. "Stuff about where she's performing."

"I can hardly hear you." Claire picked up her hairbrush. "My mother had a bad accident. She's dead."

"I know that," I said into the sheet flower. I patted the sheet flat and looked over at Claire. "I'm sorry," I told her. My mom wasn't at all dead. But still. She wasn't here. She was never here when I needed to talk about things.

Claire's blond curls bounced as she began to brush again. "I wish I'd been sick that day. If I'd been sick, she would have stayed home." She laid the brush on the bedside table and pulled her covers up to her shoulders. "She'd still be alive."

"It wasn't your fault it happened," I said. "You didn't know she was going to have an accident."

"I talk to her after I say my prayers," Claire said. "Since she's in heaven, I figure she can hear me. Do you say prayers?"

"No," I answered, and then I thought about my pretend conversations with Mom. "Actually, I talk to my mom, too," I said. "Are you done littering my room?"

She rolled her eyes and nodded.

I snapped off the light. Then, I got down beside my bed and reached under it to touch Mom's poster. I closed my eyes and thought about what to say. "Hi, Mom." My voice was a breath, not a voice. I whispered to her about my awful spring vacation and how China's growls were kind of scary.

Muffin will like you, Mom's pretty voice said inside my head.

"But she piddles," I whispered. I'd been trying all day not to think about that. Tomorrow, when I went to take care of her, I was going to have to wipe up piddle. What if I got piddle on my hand? How disgusting!

I could almost hear Mom's voice answer. It's only a week, honey, she said. And then, she surprised me. *Claire would like to be your friend*, she said.

I stiffened. Grownups never understood anything.

In the other bed, Claire was making annoying noises, whispering and breathing funny. "You better quit doing that," I said. "You better not keep me awake."

I touched Mom's poster one more time and crawled into bed. I could still hear Claire breathing. Then, I heard China growl in Tyler's room. I pulled the pillow over my head to shut everything out.

Chapter 8

China Speaks Up

Sunday morning, as I woke up, I looked
toward the wall where Mom's poster usually
hung. The wall was empty. I gasped. Then, I
remembered.

I turned my head and, sure enough, Claire
Plummer was sleeping in the other bed. Claire
Plummer, sharing my room. I peered over at her
and saw something hard sticking out from under
her pillow. In the dim light, it looked like a pencil
case. Weird. Just then, she opened her eyes.

I jumped out of bed, pretending I hadn't been looking at her.

At breakfast, Tyler reported on China. "I slept in my own bed last night," he said. "I think China likes me now."

"She's probably all adjusted now," I told him.

"She still hasn't pooped." Cheerios blew out of his mouth as he said "pooped."

"How do you know that?" Claire pushed her dish to one side, out of range.

Tyler jammed more Cheerios into his mouth and talked around them. "Her litter box doesn't have any poop in it."

Claire turned pale. "You looked in her litter box?"

Just then, a terrible noise came down the hall. A scream! High and low. And then, high again.

"That's the yowl," I said, clattering my spoon into my bowl. "That's what got her thrown out of the Motel La Paws."

"The *cat* made that racket?" Dad jumped out of his chair and ran down the hall.

We followed him.

China yowled again. She was a cat siren.
We held our hands over our ears till it stopped.
In the new silence, my ears rang with a noise
of their own.

Finally, Dad blew out a big sigh. "I hope they
can't hear that all the way to Hawaii."

"Sierra's going to be so mad about this,"
I said.

"China doesn't screech," Tyler said, snuffling,
"if I'm in here. But maybe I don't want to be in
here." He moved closer to the door. His freckles
showed up dark on his pale face.

"You HAVE to stay with her," I told him.
"That's the only way we'll get through this week.
We'll bring you toys. We'll bring everything
you need."

He crossed his arms and snuffled again.

"I'll share my candy," I said.

"Candy?" he asked.

"Yes," I said.

"And will you bring my trucks?" he asked.

"Yes," I said. "Everything you need."

"This could be good," Dad said. "We'll be

able to walk around without stepping on a truck."

Just then the phone rang, and Dad went to answer it. "It's your dad, Claire," he called.

She ran for the phone.

When she finished talking to her dad, Claire helped me gather up trucks. "Grandpa's better," she said as she piled little pickups into the back of a big dump truck, "but he's still in the hospital. I told my father about China. He said make sure she has water to drink."

China had curled into a tight ball under Tyler's bed. She growled at us as we brought in the trucks. Her eyes flashed mean lights.

Tyler moved closer to me. He shivered. "I don't like her anymore," he said.

"Want some water, China?" I asked.

She yowled again. Her awful song went up and up and flowed back down into a low rumble, sort of like thunder. She slunk out from under the bed and leapt onto Tyler's dresser. Then she scrabbled up the wall to the window sill. "Huff, huff, huff," she said. She crouched there, her ears flat to her head, her evil eyes staring. Her tail wound and unwound like a snake getting ready to strike.

A scared feeling filled my stomach. "Get Dad," I said.

China dashed toward us. We ducked as she darted between us and out the door.

We chased after her. We split up to look in every room.

"She's here," Tyler hollered from the living room. "Nope, there she goes."

Dad joined us as we raced all over trying to find her. She knocked over bottles in the kitchen. She scrabbled across Dad's newspaper on the table, sending it flying. She zipped past us one more time, headed down the hall. Then, silence.

We looked under beds, expecting that any minute she'd explode out at us. We pulled back the shower curtain and checked the bathtub. We slid closet doors open and peeked in.

No cat.

"Could she get outside?" I asked Dad.

He shook his head. "Everything's closed tight."

"She's not under my bed anymore," Tyler said. "I'm glad."

"It's worse now," I said. "Now, she could be anywhere."

As Tyler's eyes filled with tears, I realized what I'd said. "Don't worry, Tyler," I told him. "We'll find her."

But my own heart was beating too fast. My voice came out shaky.

We stood there a long time, listening. We heard nothing but our own breathing. China had vanished.

Chapter 9

Too Many Worries

*C*hina's been a pet all her life," Dad said as he
filled the tea kettle at the sink. "She wouldn't
suddenly turn wild."

"You didn't see her," I told him. "She was
creepy like a snake." I rubbed my arms where the
goose bumps still prickled. "Her face turned into
a mean tiger face. And then, she jumped at us."

Dad measured coffee grounds into a filter.
"We'll leave water and food out for her. She'll
be fine." He sniffed at the coffee grounds and
smiled. Dad loved coffee.

"Dad," I said, "you're not getting it. China hates us!"

His kettle whistled. He poured water and smiled again at his coffee grounds. It was true. He didn't get it.

A few minutes later, Tyler had driven his trucks back into every room. He honked a lot, in case China was thinking about attacking. Claire stayed in the shower for hours. Then, she sat on her bed inside a cat barricade made of pillows while she strung beads into a bracelet. I drew a jungle picture with drooling, nasty tigers that prowled through the bushes.

Dad sawed boards to make shelves for his office.

Wherever China was hiding, she was quiet. Every time I went into a new room, I looked around first to make sure she wasn't waiting to pounce. Once I was sure I saw her tail, but it was only the lamp cord.

At noon, the Andersons called to say they were leaving on their trip. At four, I had to do the first Muffin visit. "I'll come with you," Dad said.

Of course, Tyler had to come, and then, Claire went to get her jacket.

"It's my business," I told her. "You're not supposed to come."

She shook her head. "You need help," she said. "Besides, I'm sort of afraid to stay here alone." She hugged her arms around her middle and looked embarrassed. "China."

My goose bumps popped out again. "Okay," I said.

Getting Mrs. Anderson's door unlocked was the worst part, and the whole time, Muffin yapped on the other side. "Here I am," I told her once we got inside. "You can stop being a sad, lonely dog."

She climbed up my leg, panting and yapping hello. Then, she bounced around the room and left piddle drops everywhere. Feeling like Mrs. Anderson, I pushed a paper towel behind her with my foot. I had to pick it up by a little dry corner and drop it in the garbage. Dad grinned at me. "That will get easier," he said.

"I don't think so," I told him. I scrubbed my hands at the kitchen sink. Claire scrubbed

her hands, too, even though she hadn't touched
a thing.

Muffin bounced beside me as I filled her bowl
with kibble. She crunched up every bite.

"She has to go outside now," Claire said.

I sighed. "I *know* that."

"She doesn't like wet grass," Claire said.

I shook my head at Claire. Did she think I
hadn't been listening to Mrs. Anderson?

Muffin stood on the bottom porch step, lifting
one little foot and then putting it back down in the
same place. I walked onto the grass and clapped
my hands. "Come on, Muffin," I called. "See? Rain
doesn't hurt. Come on!"

Claire stuck her head out the door. "You have
to make it look like fun," she hollered. Muffin saw
the open door and rushed between Claire's feet to
go back inside.

"Now, I have to do it all over again," I yelled.
"Just stay inside Claire." It took ages, but finally
I got Muffin out on the grass.

"Good doggy," I said. "This is the right place
to piddle. On the grass. Not the floor."

She shook herself and ran back onto the porch. Had she piddled? I hoped so. When we got back inside, I threw the ball for her until finally she flopped down and panted.

"Don't worry about a thing," I told her. "We'll play every day." She licked my hand with her pink tongue. Dad laughed as he put down the book he'd been reading to Tyler. "She's your friend now. Good job, Katie."

As I picked up the key, Muffin's tail drooped. She looked up at me with dark, sad eyes. "We have to take her home," I told Dad. "Look how sad she is."

Dad shook his head. "We have a cat," he said. "That's more than enough."

After I locked the door, Dad said I could take care of Muffin without him the next morning. He'd do the night visits.

Back at home, I hung Mrs. Anderson's key on the hook. If it weren't for the "excitement drops," taking care of Muffin would be easy.

That night Claire asked me to play Concentration.

"Watch out," Dad said with a grin. "She's good."

He was right. I couldn't believe how well she remembered where the cards were. "Tomorrow, we play a different game," I told her. "Parcheesi."

"Good," Claire said. "That's my favorite."

As we got ready for bed, I couldn't stop thinking about China. Was she hungry? Thirsty? And what was I going to tell Sierra? That her cat hated my house so much it turned into a monster cat and ran away?

"Do you think Dad is right?" I asked Claire. "That China will be okay?"

Claire set down her brush. "Does he know much about cats?"

"No," I answered.

"When I say my prayers," Claire said, "I'll say one for China."

I turned out the light. China wasn't under my bed; I'd already checked. I knelt and touched Mom's poster. "Dear Mom," I whispered, and I told her about China, and how she'd scared us. But I was also worried. "Do you think she'll be okay?" I asked. "How will she eat?"

Mom seemed worried, too. *Maybe she'll come out tomorrow*, she said. As I climbed into bed, I heard Claire whispering. I wondered what she and her mother talked about.

As I settled back into my pillow, I listened again for sounds of China. All I heard was Dad's game on TV. Was China creeping around the house, mad at us? Sharpening her claws so she could scratch us? I pulled the covers over my head, just in case.

Chapter 10

Claire Writes Things Down

On Monday morning, my alarm went off just like on school days. I dragged out of bed, wishing Muffin was a late sleeper. Claire jumped up and was dressed in two minutes.

"Hurry up," she said.

"Huh?" I said. "You're not going."

"You need me with you," she said, "to help you. You could hardly unlock that door, Katie."

I ran into Dad's room. He was sleeping! "Dad," I said to the big lump in the bed. "Claire says she's going with me to take care of Muffin."

"Good idea," he mumbled. He turned over and started to snore.

I gave up. I tried to run ahead of Claire to Mrs. Anderson's house, but she caught up with me when the key stuck in the lock. Muffin yapped on the other side of the door. "I'm coming, Muffin," I yelled. She barked even louder.

When I finally got the door open, Muffin came running. And piddling. She raced between the kitchen and the family room. Her little legs sped across the carpet and then stiffened into a skid every time she reached the slippery kitchen floor. I held my nose and cleaned up the excitement drops.

As I poured food into Muffin's dish, she bounced up and down and pushed her furry white face into the dish before I was even done. "You like your food better than me," I said. I crouched down beside her and watched her get crumbs all over her face.

After Muffin tiptoed around the backyard and pooped, I sat on the kitchen floor and played guess-which-leg-I'm-hiding-the-ball-under. Claire

sat at the kitchen table, writing in a notebook.
My notebook!

"What are you doing?" I asked.

"Writing things," she said.

"Why?" I asked.

"It's how you run a business," she said. "You
write things down." She tapped her pencil on the
notebook. "How come you know how to play with
Muffin?" she asked.

I tossed the ball again, and Muffin scooted
after it. She brought it back, tossing it in the
air, like a circus dog. "It's Tyler," I said finally.
"A little brother is sort of like a pet."

Claire made a face. "Tyler," she said, "is loud.
And messy. You can hardly walk through all the
trucks and blocks and stuff in your house."

I pictured Claire's shiny kitchen counters
and vacuumed rugs. Sometimes, I wished our
house didn't look so much like a day care center.
I sighed.

Muffin crawled into my lap and curled up
like a baby. When I rubbed her belly she kicked
her back leg and grinned at me. "Sweet doggy,"

I crooned. Her eyes closed and she began
to snore.

When we got back home, Dad, wearing his
robe, was finishing a phone call. He waved his
hand at me. "The woman who lives around the
corner," he said, "has fish that need to be fed.
Her name is Ruby. I know she's a nice person,
so I told her you'd do it."

Did I want another customer? Muffin was
fun. China was not. I pictured a bowl of goldfish.
How hard could that be?

Chapter 11

Fish, Fish, and More Fish

I made Claire give back my notebook before we went to the fish lady's house.

"I've heard she tells fortunes," Claire said. "I think she has a crystal ball."

As Ruby opened her door, her silky, purple robes billowed around her. A gold tiara sparkled on her dark, curly hair. When she closed the door, gold curtains shimmered against the walls. Beads glittered from the edges of lampshades. More beads rattled in the doorways.

"What's that nice smell?" Dad asked as Tyler reached for a green-and-blue feather that waved from a tall vase on the floor. Dad shook his head and picked him up.

"Incense," she answered. "Here, little boy. Would you like a peacock feather?" She pulled one from the vase, waved it like a wand, and handed it to Tyler. Her fingers sparkled with rings.

"Are you a fairy princess?" Tyler stared at her, his eyes round.

"Not a bit, sweetheart," Ruby answered. "I wish I were. Then, all our wishes would come true." She smiled. "Let's go see my fish." Her skirts drifted out like purple clouds as she rustled through a bead curtain. We rustled after her.

All at once, we were surrounded by bubbling water and beautiful fish. Goldfish swam in bowls on the tables, but most of Ruby's fish were in big tanks. In one tank, a big fish, bigger than a sandwich, lumbered through tall grasses and herded smaller fish, black and orange, in and out of a castle. The tank at the back wall held a curled-up pink shell. Fish darted like silver arrows and then huddled inside the shell as if they were having a quick party. In a third tank, a pancake-shaped fish drifted across blue sand while black-and-white striped fish played tag around it.

Watery lights rippled in Dad's glasses. "This is more than I expected," he said in a worried voice.

As Ruby touched her finger to the glass of one tank, the fish gathered. They waved their fins at her. Their mouths opened and closed as if they were talking. "Hello, hello," Ruby crooned.

"Katie's only nine," Dad said in that same worried voice.

I hugged my notebook close to my chest. Ruby's fish belonged in the aquarium at the coast. They were *not* a couple of goldfish.

Ruby turned then, and held out her hands to Claire and me. I drew in my breath. Then, I stepped forward and rested one hand in Ruby's as Claire took her other hand. Ruby knelt so her face was close. I stared at the sparkles on her eyelids.

One sparkle had dropped onto her cheek. She smelled like flowers.

"The person I usually call is out of town," Ruby said, speaking to both of us in a low voice. "I have to be gone till Friday." She gently squeezed our hands and tipped her head as if listening to something. She spoke again. "This is something you can do. I can tell you are people who love fish."

I pressed Ruby's hand in return. "I'm the one," I said. "Claire's just visiting."

Ruby smiled. "Isn't it nice," she said, "that you have a good helper? I'm glad there will be two of you."

I sighed. "Okay," I said. "Two of us."

Ruby stood up in a swirl of purple silk. She took a box of fish food off the shelf. "They need this much, once a day." She showed us how much she poured in her hand. Then she brushed the food off her hand and into one of the tanks. As soon as the food touched the water, the fish splashed and zipped around.

"Wow!" I said. "The little one grabbed a piece away from the big one."

"I named that big one," Ruby said. "He's Harry Truman."

"After the President?" Dad asked.

Ruby shook her head. "After the man who wouldn't leave his home when the volcano erupted."

I nodded. Every time we drove to Portland and saw Mount St. Helens, someone would tell that story. I'd heard about that man a million times.

"Harry Truman was a tough, old guy," Dad said. "This fish looks tough and old, too."

Ruby watched me measure food and sprinkle it into one of the other tanks.

"Ahem," Dad said as I moved toward the third tank. Oh yes. Stupid Claire. Did I have to include her? I moved again toward the tank. Then, I stopped and held the fish food can out to her. I had to bump the can against her arm before she noticed me.

"Everything is beautiful," she said in a soft voice as she finally took the can. She held the can a moment, staring at the fish, her face glowing in the soft light. At last, she measured out food and sprinkled it into the third tank.

Ruby smiled at her. "I was sure you'd be good at this."

While Claire dropped food into the goldfish bowls, I wrote in the notebook. Ruby handed me a house key that had a feather and a crystal hanging from it.

Claire nudged me. "Emergency," she whispered.

"I'm doing it," I said. I turned to Ruby. "Who should we call if something goes wrong?"

Ruby sighed and nodded. "Sometimes, things go wrong." She looked up the number of the fish store, and as I wrote it down, I thought of China. Sometimes, things *did* go wrong.

Beside me, Dad shifted Tyler to his other arm. "What about the mail?" he asked.

Ruby led us into the front hall. "It comes through that slot in the door," she said. "Perhaps you could put it on the table?"

"Mail on table," I wrote.

"Ruby has a lot of fish," I said as we started

back home. "But we only have to come once a day. All we have to do is sprinkle food on their water."

"I'm going to hang beads on all my lampshades at home," Claire said, "and get some feathers to put in vases. And wear prettier clothes."

"The best one is the hairy turnip one," Tyler said.

"Harry Truman," I said.

"China would like those fish," Tyler said. "If she ever comes back."

Dad shook his head. "It's odd we haven't heard that cat. Or seen her."

Claire stepped around a swampy place in the yard and tiptoed back toward us through the squishy grass. Her eyes were shining. "I didn't know this until just now," she said, "but I'm going to get a pet. My pet will be a beautiful fish."

Chapter 12

Where is China Cat?

We need to make a business calendar," Claire said later that morning. "We can write down all the things we have to do."

"We don't need a calendar," I said.

"Think of it," Claire said. "We can make it seven pages long—a page for each day. Every day will have a list in it."

I thought about it. Maybe Claire's idea was okay, after all. "It has to be very big," I said. "We'll put it up on the wall." I ran to get my construction paper and colored pens. We divided each day into Morning, Afternoon, and Night.

"We have two pets," I said. "Let's use a different color for each."

Claire looked at me with her eyebrows raised high. "Three," she said.

"Huh?"

"Three pets."

I groaned as I remembered China Cat. "But there's nothing we can do about her, except look for her."

"We'll write that in," Claire said. "LOOK FOR CHINA."

"Muffin stuff is three times a day," I said. "Our calendar will get really full. It's going to look great."

"The fish have to be in purple," Claire said, picking through my markers, "because that's Ruby's favorite color."

I sighed. "It's my business," I reminded her.

"The calendar was my idea," she said.

I frowned at her. "China will be red," I said. "Sierra's favorite color."

"Make Muffin blue," Tyler said. "And read everything to me."

Claire picked up the purple marker. FEED THE FISH, she printed in the middle of each morning square.

I wrote in blue, FEED MUFFIN, for every morning and every afternoon. Then, I wrote THROW THE BALL. PLAY HIDE AND SEEK. WIPE UP PIDDLE. I put a frowny face next to "piddle."

FIND CHINA, Claire wrote in red marker. She set the marker down.

"There's not enough red," Tyler said.

"We have to do more for China," I said, trying to swallow over the terrible lump in my throat. "We have to stop being afraid of her. We've got to turn her back into a pet."

"Write BRING HER A TOY," Tyler said. "And SING HER A SONG."

"How can we?" Claire asked. "We don't know where she is."

"We'll do it where she *maybe* is," Tyler said. "We'll go different places and do it."

I picked up the red marker and began to write.

When we finished, the calendar looked really important. We taped it onto the family room wall.

At eleven, I filled China's water dish. "Come for your water," I called. "Nice kitty." I thunked her water dish three times with a spoon. Would she hear her dish? Would she come out? If she came, would she leap at me? I waited. Nothing happened.

At one, Claire filled China's food dish. She went into every room, waving the empty can in the air. "Dinner for China," she sang.

No cat.

At three, Tyler decided she was behind the couch even though we'd looked there a hundred times. He sang a long song to the couch. China never answered.

At four o'clock, when it was time to take care of Muffin, Claire came along.

"If you're going to be a business partner," I said, "you have to do half the work." I handed her a paper towel.

She jumped back. "No piddle!" she said. "I'll feed her."

"No way," I answered. "That's the best part!"

She ended up doing nothing, except for writing in the notebook. Before we came home, I taught Muffin a trick. I'd say "Give me a kiss," and she'd lick my cheek with her cute pink tongue. She even licked Claire's cheek. Of course, Claire had to scrub it right off with a tissue.

After dinner, Claire and I got out the Parcheesi board.

Tyler sat near us with his construction paper and his blunt scissors. "China will like these," he said. He held up a paper fish. "I'm going to leave these fish in all the good cat places," he said.

"Where are the good cat places?" Claire asked.

"I'm finding them," he said. He bent over the fish he was cutting. "They're still a secret."

I sighed and threw the dice. "I wish China hadn't turned into a wild cat."

"You just missed a good play," Claire said. "Pay attention to the game."

"Is Sierra going to be mad?" Tyler asked.

I nodded. "Her cat is ruined. Sierra will never be my friend again."

"You can get pen pals," Claire said. "Pen pals are very interesting."

"I don't want pen pals," I said. "Sierra and I have been best friends forever. Since day care."

Claire landed on my space and sent me home. Then, she won. Tomorrow we'd choose a different game.

"I wonder where Ruby keeps her crystal ball," Claire said as we got ready for bed. "I wonder if she can tell the future."

"She probably has a magic broom," I said. "We could find it and drive it around."

"That's ridiculous," Claire said. "Brooms aren't really magic. But I think crystal balls are."

"I hope nothing goes wrong with her fish," I said. "If she's magic, she could turn us into mice. And then, China would get us."

Claire clattered her brush onto the bedside table. "Can we close your bedroom door right now?" she asked.

"Why?"

"China might come in here." Claire's eyes were wide. "I keep remembering the way she yowled. It was like a horror movie scream."

I shivered. "We don't know where she is. What if she's . . . ?"

Claire clenched her hands together. "Already in here?"

We jumped off the beds and checked the whole room. Even the closet. No evil eyes stared out at us. Nothing hissed at us. We closed the door tight and jumped back into bed.

Chapter 13

China is Everywhere

I n the middle of the night, something made
my eyes pop open. The street light outside
my window made shadows cross my closet door.
I listened hard.

"I heard something," Claire's voice said from
the other bed.

"Me, too." My teeth chattered as I spoke.

"Daddy," a little voice called. "Daddy!" We
heard Tyler's feet thump on the floor and run into
Dad's room.

The sound came again. A growl. Right there in my room. Right between Claire and me! I leaped out of bed and flew through the door, with Claire behind me. We jumped onto Dad's bed just as he was turning on the light.

"She's in my room," I said.

"No," Tyler said, "she's under my bed." He shuddered and crawled into Dad's arms. "I don't like her under there."

Just then, a mutter, a mean, mad sound, came from across the room. "She's in here," Claire said, jumping up and down on the bed. "Right THERE." She pointed to a spot under the window.

We stared. Nothing was there. Nothing at all.

All at once, Dad smiled. "The heat duct," he said. "Could China be talking through the heat ducts?" He saw my face. "Those metal ducts go under the house and branch up into every room," he said. "If she's near any one of them, they'd carry her voice all over the house."

We were silent as the muttering went on and on. I tiptoed to the place where heat came into Dad's room. I tapped the metal grate that covered the hole. "China," I called. "Can you hear me?"

The muttering stopped.

"Go to bed," I called. "It's the middle of the night." I looked at the others. "Maybe she doesn't know that," I explained.

"One good thing," Dad said. "She's alive. And we haven't lost her."

"But if she's wild," I said, "she might come out and get us."

"That's not going to happen," Dad said. He looked at me with his special look that meant, "Stop scaring Tyler."

"Time for us to hit the hay," he said. He yawned. "It's the middle of the night, as you just pointed out."

"I'm staying with you, Daddy," Tyler said.

Dad sighed. Claire and I went back to my room. We left the door open. Why not? We couldn't keep China out. She was everywhere.

Chapter 14

Tyler Speaks Up

On Tuesday morning, after Claire and I fed Muffin, we walked to Ruby's house. After we fed the fish, we sat on the floor of the fish room, watching them. They were better than TV. They moved like acrobats as they twisted and dove through the water.

After a while, I checked the time. "We have to go," I told Claire. "We have to do a China thing."

Claire stood up with a sigh. "If I could find Ruby's crystal ball," she said, "it might tell us where China is hiding."

"We're not supposed to look around other people's houses," I said. "Dad said so."

"I'll just look here and there," Claire said. She walked in slow motion to the front door, turning her head back and forth. "She probably keeps it in her bedroom," she said. "I'd love to see Ruby's bedroom."

"We have to go," I said. I held the door open.

Once we got outside, Claire glided home, pretending she was swimming through the air.

Dad met us at the door. "Did Tyler go with you?"

We shook our heads.

"He must be here then," Dad said. "I have to warn you. China's talking a lot."

I stopped with my jacket half off, half on. "Did you see her?"

He shook his head.

Just then, an eerie yowl came out of the heat duct in the family room and, at the same time, from somewhere in the living room. The whole house echoed with China's yowl. I covered my ears. "She sounds like TWO cats."

"I might have known." Dad strode down the hall. "Tyler," he called.

"Meooow,"said a voice that sounded a little bit like Tyler.

"Meeeeeooooow,"said another voice that came out of the heat ducts. That one had to be China.

"Come out," Dad said in a stern voice.

Tyler's face, bright red, peeked out from under his bed. Claire covered her eyes as he flashed the flashlight in her face.

"I've looked everywhere for you," Dad said. "Why didn't you answer?"

"I did," Tyler said. He clicked the light at me and crawled back under the bed. "Meeooow," he said.

"Meooow," all the heat ducts answered. And then we heard, "Huff, huff, huff."

"Huff, huff, huff," Tyler said.

"I don't understand," Claire said in a little voice.

"There's a heat duct under that bed," Dad explained. "They're taking to each other through the ducts." As he turned toward the door, he raised his voice. "I'll be in my office, Tyler," he called, "in case you need me."

Evil hisses came from under the bed. I clapped my hands again over my ears, but the sounds were too loud. All over the house, the heat ducts began to hiss.

There was no safe place.

Claire "Fixes" Things

When I asked Dad, he said, "No. Absolutely not." We could *not* move to a motel.

"How about my house?" Claire asked.

"Thanks, but we're staying here," Dad said. "This is our home."

"Some home," I said. "Haunted."

Claire and I gave up on Dad and went into my bedroom.

"I've got to do something besides think about China," I told her. "Muffin would like some rain boots. I'll make them out of the cloth on my broken umbrella."

"I'm going to make something very beautiful," Claire said. "A necklace to wear to Ruby's house." She reached for her bead box.

All afternoon, Tyler crept around the house with the flashlight. He and China kept on hissing. "Quit that," I told Tyler. But he wouldn't stop.

At four o'clock, we took Muffin's boots to her. Muffin chewed them right off. "You'll have wet feet then," I told her as I let her into the yard.

"Let's go home, Claire," I said when we came back in. "I figured out how to make these boots better."

She looked up from writing in the notebook. "I got it all," she said. "Muffin happy to see us. Ate all her food. Hated her boots. Pooped in the back yard. Katie didn't throw the ball."

"You don't have to write THAT." I said.

"You're supposed to exercise her. Today, you didn't."

"I don't have to throw the ball every time."

Claire made another note. "I hope she doesn't start to gain weight."

"One time of not throwing the ball? She's going to gain weight?"

"You know what else?" Claire pointed at the Mrs. Anderson's refrigerator. "They have a dentist appointment coming up. See that little bitty paper?"

"So?"

"You can hardly see that paper. I bet they forget to go."

"It's not our business, Claire." Muffin drank water and sneezed it on my arm. I filled up her bowl and set it on the floor. "Let's go."

"You know what else?" she asked.

I patted Muffin's silky ears while I waited.

Claire tucked the notebook under her arm and poked her finger into the dirt around Mrs. Anderson's leafy house plant on the table. "I bet she wanted us to water this."

"I'm going to lock you in if you don't come," I said.

"I can move it so it'll get more light," she said. "Be . . . gonia glori . . . osa," she read from a little tag. "Look how it's drooping."

"I don't think you should move things,"
I said.

Claire watered the plant and thumped it
onto the floor under a lamp. She glanced at the
refrigerator door again. "I'll need to fix that
dentist thing too," she said. "Tomorrow, I'll put
a blue arrow on the refrigerator. I'll make it point
to that little paper."

I rolled my eyes. As I picked up the house
key, Muffin's tail drooped to the floor and she
looked ready to cry. "Poor baby," I said. "If we
didn't have a crazy cat living with us, we'd take
you home." Claire and I took turns giving Muffin
twenty-six more pats while we said the alphabet.
By the time we got to Z, Muffin's eyes sparkled
and her tail waved like a happy flag.

That night, Claire wanted to play Parcheesi
again. I beat her. The first time I'd won. Of
course, Claire had to point that out.

The whole time we played, we could hear
China muttering. Tyler kept sneaking around,
going from heat duct to heat duct. "She's loudest
here," he called once from the kitchen.

Dad showed me how to close the heat duct between our beds. "I can't figure out where she is," he said. "She can't be inside the ducts. They're sealed."

"So, where is she?" I asked.

He shook his head. "I don't know."

Claire and I folded a blanket over the heat duct. After that, we could hardly hear China's voice.

The rest of bedtime was the same. Claire nodded at me when she finished brushing her hair. I turned out the light and then knelt down beside my bed to talk to Mom's poster.

"The week's going by, Mom," I whispered to the poster. "It's Tuesday. Taking care of Muffin is fun." I waited. Mom didn't answer.

"Will we ever find China?" I asked.

No answer.

"Is Sierra going to hate me?"

No answer.

I sighed and climbed into bed.

Chapter 16

Disaster!

Wednesday morning, a little bit of sun peeked through the clouds. The wet leaves in the yard sparkled at us. "I forgot to work on Muffin's boots," I said as we slogged across the wet yard.

"She's not barking," Claire said. "That's nicer."

"Maybe this time, she won't piddle," I said. I pushed the door open. "Muffin," I called. "Where are you?"

Silence.

"Claire," I said.

She looked at me, her eyes scared. Then, we heard a strange wheezing. We tiptoed toward the sound.

Muffin lay under the kitchen table. Her feet and legs twitched. Her eyes were closed. The white fur around her mouth was green!

Beside her on the floor I saw a thick, green puddle. Another green puddle was by the chair. Claire knelt next to me. We stared at Muffin's green lips.

I touched Muffin's head and felt sticky fur. She pushed out her tongue. Her tongue was green. I swallowed, trying not to throw up.

Claire pointed at something. Then, she burst into tears.

The plant.

The plant she'd moved to the floor stood with naked stems. The green puddles on the floor held clumps of leaves. Claire grabbed my arm, her sharp nails sinking into my skin.

"Get Dad," I told her.

She ran out the door.

Dad came fast, carrying Tyler. He set Tyler in Mrs. Anderson's rocker, squatted down beside Muffin, and stroked her back. "Hey, little girl," he said softly. "Got a belly ache?"

Muffin's tail moved a tiny bit. That was all.

Dad's forehead wrinkled up with worry. He went to the phone. "I'll call the vet," he said. "We'll probably have to take her in."

It took forever for him to dial. Then, he waited while someone talked to the vet. "I'm on hold," he said. He blew out a long breath and pressed the phone hard against his ear.

I touched Muffin's head with my finger. Would she ever give kisses again? Would she toss the ball in the air like a circus dog? I touched her again. Would she die?

At last, someone came back on the phone. We heard a voice, talking and talking. "Yes," Dad kept saying, and then, "Yes, we will."

Finally, he hung up and turned to us. "The vet said throwing up was good for her. She may throw up again if she needs to. She says Muffin should feel better in a few hours." Dad stepped around a green puddle and looked at the stubby plant on the floor. "She said to keep her away from plants."

Claire burst into tears again.

"Begonia gloriosa?" Dad set the plant on the table. "Not so gloriosa anymore."

"You're going to get in big trouble," Tyler said.

"What do you mean?" I asked.

"That was her prize," Tyler said. "At the County Fair. She told me."

"Oh, dear," Dad said. "It's probably special then." He pulled paper towels off the roll. "Right now, we have to clean this up."

After we cleaned the kitchen, Dad held Muffin gently in his arms and washed her face and her paws under the faucet. I patted her dry while Claire made her a clean bed.

"We still have to do the fish," I told Dad. "Is it okay to leave Muffin alone?"

"You should check on her every hour," Dad said, "until she gets back to feeling perky."

"I'll do it," Claire said.

"I'll come too," I said. Every hour, Muffin. Every other hour, China. This spring vacation was ruled by clocks. We might as well be at school! I pictured Sierra at the beach, running in and out

of the waves. Eating ice cream bars in the warm
sunshine.

Dad and Tyler went home. The sun was gone
by then, and cold rain drizzled on us as Claire and
I dragged ourselves to Ruby's house. The fish
swirled around, happy to see us. They trust us, I
thought, even though we don't really know how
to take care of them. I wished Dad had come to
Ruby's with us.

After we fed the fish, we hunkered down to
watch them. Harry Truman's big lips kissed the
wall of the tank and then he flipped his tail and
wandered to the other side. All the other fish
parted to let him through.

"Muffin trusted us," I said.

Claire hiccupped and turned to me. "If she
had died, it would be all my fault." She gulped
and swallowed hard.

"China is crazy now," I said, "and that's
my fault."

"If only I hadn't moved that plant," Claire
said. Her blue eyes filled up with tears and
overflowed.

"Mrs. Anderson probably didn't know that plant is poison, either," I said. But part of me knew Claire was right. At least, she was admitting she shouldn't have moved it. I shifted my bottom on the floor and hugged my knees against my chest. "I hate being a pet sitter," I said. "I'll never, ever do it again."

"Me, too," she said.

We watched the fish until we had to go. Watching them was the only thing that made us feel better.

Chapter 17

More Trouble

By Thursday, the only reminder of Muffin's sickness was the green fur around her mouth. "Mrs. Anderson's coming home tomorrow," I told Claire. "I wish Muffin's face wasn't green."

"Let's try toothpaste," Claire said. "It makes teeth whiter. Maybe it works on dog hair."

I ran home to get our toothpaste. We held Muffin over the kitchen sink and rubbed the stuff into her fur. At first, she smacked her lips, then she twisted her head away. Then, she sneezed and shook her head until her ears almost flew off. "I give up," I said. I set her down on the floor.

"Now look," Claire said. "The window over the sink has toothpaste spattered all over it."

I sighed. "Everything we do turns out awful."

Claire rubbed at the window while I tried to pat Muffin's face with a towel. When I finally stopped, she zipped around the room in happy circles. Then she finished her face by rubbing it all over the rug.

"Mrs. Anderson is going to be so mad about the plant," Claire said. "Her begonia gloriosa. Her prize."

I stared at the plant. Only a few shredded leaves still hung from the ugly stalks. I could see Muffin's tooth marks on them. "Let's go," I said.

As we started for Ruby's house, I pulled my hood over my head. Raining again. Claire, of course, had her boots and her umbrella. "I'm worried about Tyler, too," I said.

"He keeps talking cat talk into the heat ducts," Claire said. "Creeping around with that flashlight. He's really strange."

My tennis shoes sank into a puddle and ice water seeped in the sides. "Dad says China must be drinking water from somewhere. Her dish never gets empty. He said maybe she comes to drink out of the toilet in the middle of the night."

"Euw!" Claire stopped twirling the umbrella.

"If she drinks, at least she's not dying!"

"I can't believe Sierra loves that cat," Claire said.

"She used to be sweet," I said. "She used to wind herself around my legs and hold her head up for a pat." I wasn't making that up, but now, I could hardly believe it had ever happened.

At Ruby's, Claire sorted the mail into Junk and Not Junk. "Ruby gets the strangest mail!" she said as she read from a flyer. "Talk again with your lost loved ones. Meet us in Paradise, Montana for a heavenly experience."

"I wonder if Ruby will go to that," I said. I swished through the bead curtain into the fish room. "If she does, I hope she doesn't ask us to fish sit."

We sprinkled exactly the right amount of food into the tanks and the bowls, and then hunkered down to watch the fish.

Claire opened the notebook and began to write. "At least, nothing bad has happened at Ruby's house," she said.

"Wait a minute," I said. I leaped up to peer into the biggest tank. Harry Truman lay on the bottom. On his side.

Stiff as a board.

Dead.

Chapter 18

"You Were a Good Swimmer"

The phone at home rang and rang. Finally I remembered Dad wasn't there. He'd made Tyler go with him. They were running errands.

"Call the fish store," Claire said. She found the number in our notebook.

The fish store person said get Harry Truman out of the tank in case he had something infectious. We should dispose of him, the man said.

"Dispose?" I asked.

"Bury him or something." The man sounded busy. He hung up.

"Can we get him out with this?" Claire stood on her tiptoes to reach a net Ruby had hung near the tanks.

I pulled a chair close to the tank and stood on it. When I dipped the net in, the fish darted about, splashing, practically leaping out. I pulled the net back. "What will we do?"

"They're slowing down," Claire said. "Go in again. Go a little at a time."

I lowered the net little by little into the water. The handle was too short. I had to push my whole arm into the water. Slowly.

"Your sleeve's getting wet." Claire made a face.

"They're bumping me," I said, "with their heads."

"They think you're food," Claire said. "Good thing they have little mouths."

Finally, in slow motion, my net touched Harry. His body drifted away.

Claire pushed her face against the glass side of the tank and I could see her nose squashed flat. The other fish gathered around her nose. Claire blinked and pulled back.

At last, I got the net under Harry. I pulled him to the top, but then, all at once, he weighed a ton. It took both hands to get him out of the water. "Quick," I yelled. "Get something."

Claire ran out of the room and slammed cupboard doors in Ruby's kitchen. She came back with a plate. I slid Harry onto it. He lay there, looking like dinner.

"We have to save him for Ruby," Claire said. She carried the plate to the dining room table.

"He might stink," I said. "Dad forgot to put fish in the refrigerator once."

"That's it," Claire said. "We'll put Harry in the refrigerator."

She picked up the plate. Too fast. Harry slid off, skated across the table, and smacked onto the floor. Claire screamed as the fishy body slid across the floor and bumped into Ruby's stereo.

"Get him," she screeched. "Oh, get him."

"Lucky he didn't break," I said. It took two plates to get Harry scooped up again. I balanced him on one of the plates and made it back to the table. "Look at his mouth," I said. "He doesn't look happy."

"I know exactly what to do," Claire said. She grabbed her raincoat and pushed her arms into the sleeves. "Ruby would want us to have a real funeral. With flowers and singing. And we'll say nice things about Harry. You don't know about funerals, Katie. But I do."

I stared at her. "This is a fish, Claire," I said finally. "This is different from people."

But she wouldn't listen. She raced out the front door.

I touched Harry's stiff tail. Why was he dead? Had we done something wrong?

A few minutes later, Claire came back in the house with bunches of red berries and leaves. We heaped them on the plate around Harry and even tucked some underneath to hold him in place.

I wedged more berries around his head as thoughts of Ruby kept coming. Ruby not smiling. Ruby yelling at us.

Claire stepped back and nodded at Harry. "Now, we say good things about this poor fish." She pressed her hands together and her face got very sad. "Like . . . you were always kind to little fish."

I swallowed. What could I say?

"Um, . . . you were a good swimmer," I said.

Claire waited.

I shrugged and shook my head.

"Now, we sing," Claire said.

"We need Tyler for this," I said, but all at once, I knew the best song. "Row, row, row your boat," I sang. Claire smiled at me and joined in. We sang it three times – slow, fast, and slow again. When we were done, we slid Harry into Ruby's refrigerator between the yogurt and the carrot juice.

We stood a moment, cold air rushing out at us. Harry looked great!

"Life," Claire said, "is but a dream." She shut the refrigerator door.

"What about Ruby?" I asked.

"We could write her a note," Claire said.

I opened my notebook. "Dear Ruby," I wrote.

"Tell her we're very sad," Claire said. "Tell her he's in the refrigerator." She peered over my shoulder. "You're spelling refrigerator wrong."

"I think Harry Truman died because he was old," I said, putting down the pencil. "But I'm not sure. Every one of the pets has had something awful happen."

Claire stepped back and stared at me. "We did everything right. I never looked for her crystal ball. I didn't move one plant."

"But maybe there was something. . . ." I stopped as fear filled up my stomach.

"That settles it," Claire said. "I'm *never* going to have pets. No fish. No nothing."

I shook my head at her. "This doesn't have anything to do with . . ."

"Things go wrong," Claire said. "They die."

"But . . . ," I started to say, and then I looked at Claire's face, tight and pale. We left Ruby's note on the table and walked home.

My house was strangely quiet as we let ourselves in. Tyler poked his head out of his room.

"You're back," I said. "Did you help Dad run errands?"

"Meow," Tyler answered.

"Don't be silly, Tyler."

"Meow," he answered and backed into his room. Claire and I followed him in.

"What's all over you?" I asked. "You're filthy. You've got cobwebs in your hair."

He didn't answer. He wiggled under his bed, and we squatted down to look under there.

Tyler turned toward us. He opened his mouth. "YEEEOOOUUUUWL," he said.

It sounded like China's yowl. Coming out of Tyler.

I leaped back and bumped into Claire.

"YEEEOOOUUUUWL," came a sound from all over the house. It echoed out of every heat duct – from the bathroom, the living room, the kitchen and Dad's bedroom.

I clapped my hands over my ears. "Quit that," I yelled.

In the sudden quiet, I pounded my fist on Tyler's bed. "You're asking for it, Tyler. You're in big trouble."

I heard my breath go in and out, too fast.

"Huff, huff, huff," Tyler's voice said.

Or did it come out of the heat ducts?

I didn't know.

Chapter 19

Facing Mrs. Anderson

The phone rang.

"It's probably your dad," I said to Claire. He'd been calling her every day.

Claire ran to answer the phone, but a moment later, I heard her voice say, "I'll get Katie." She sucked in her breath as she handed the phone to me.

"We're home," Mrs. Anderson's voice said into my ear. "A day early. The grandchildren wore us to a frazzle."

"Oh, good," I answered. Tomorrow morning we could sleep in. No more Muffin care.

"I'm very upset," her voice continued, "about what I found here."

My hand stuck to the phone. I could hardly breathe.

"When you bring the key back," Mrs. Anderson said, "I expect some explanations."

Claire and I marched across the yard like we were marching to the electric chair.

Mrs. Anderson met us at the door with Muffin in her arms. Claire started talking the moment the door opened.

"It was my fault," she said. "She threw up all over the place. It was all my fault."

"We called the vet," I said. "I mean, Dad called the vet. The vet said throwing up was okay."

Mrs. Anderson held her hands up. "Come in," she said. "And slow down."

We told her the whole story.

She sat in her rocker, holding Muffin close to her, like a baby. "I was upset about my plant," she said. "I didn't know Muffin got sick." She touched Muffin's green fur. "I see," she said.

She rocked Muffin back and forth, blinking

her eyes, trying not to cry. "We get so attached to pets," she said finally. "The plant isn't important."

"I thought it needed more light." Claire shoved her hands into her jacket pockets. "Katie told me not to move it."

Mrs. Anderson nodded. "It did need more light. I was going to do something about that. I probably would have put it in the same place."

Claire drew a deep breath. "Really?" she asked.

"I had no idea Muffin would eat a plant," Mrs. Anderson said. "She's never done that before." She touched Muffin's green fur. Muffin licked her hand. Then, she set Muffin on the floor and picked up her purse.

"No money," I said. I moved toward the door. "We don't deserve money."

Claire put her hands behind her back.

"But you worked hard," Mrs. Anderson said. "In my opinion, you really earned this money." She gave each of us a five-dollar bill. Then, she even hugged us and gave us some peppermint candy she found in her purse.

"She doesn't hate us," I said as we crossed the yard to go home.

"She sort of seemed to *like* us," Claire said. "I don't get it."

That night, when Tyler showed up for dinner, he tried to eat his pasta by putting his mouth in his plate and sucking. When Dad scolded him, Tyler meowed. He hissed when Dad offered ice cream. After that, he crawled down the hall on his hands and knees.

Dad kept shaking his head as he scooped ice cream into dishes for Claire and me.

"Tyler's crazy, too," I said. I wondered again where China was hiding.

After dessert, Claire and I played Checkers. She beat me two out of three. "Tomorrow, we play Sorry," I told her.

"I love Sorry," Claire said.

I sighed.

Just before we turned out the light, Claire said, "I'm glad I didn't go to Washington, D.C."

"You're kidding." I turned to look at her. "We had green throw-up. A crazy cat. A dead Harry Truman."

"It was very interesting." She closed her notebook and put it on the bedside table. "I'm ready to pray," she said.

First, we made sure China was not in my room. Claire closed the door while I straightened the blanket on top of the heat duct. It got cold in my room with no heat coming in, but at least, we wouldn't hear China. I turned out the light and slid out of bed and onto my knees. My talk with Mom's poster was short. "I can't wait for spring vacation to be over," I whispered. In my whole life, I'd never said THAT!

I pushed my forehead against my bed and thought about what to say next. "Claire is sort of okay," I whispered very softly.

What was I saying? Was I going crazy, too? I climbed back into bed, disgusted.

Chapter 20

China—Still Wild

Friday morning, after we got back from feeding Ruby's fish, Tyler had disappeared. "I've looked everywhere," Dad told us. He raised his voice. "Young man," he said, "you're in big trouble." He lowered his voice. "He's hiding," he told us. "I've been putting up my shelves, but I keep hearing him."

We followed him into his office.

"I finally have room for all those files that were stacked in the closet," he told us. He slid his closet door open and then turned back with a surprised look. "Who's been in here?" he asked. "I had things sorted into piles."

Claire and I peered around him into the closet. "Not me," I said.

"Me," a little voice said. There in the back of Dad's closet stood Tyler with dust bunnies on his sweatshirt. "I was playing," he said.

"In my closet?"

"Under it," Tyler answered in that same little voice. He clicked the flashlight off and on. Then he hid the light behind his back and brushed at a dust bunny on his knee.

Dad stepped into the closet. "What do you mean—*under* it?" Then he stepped back out, shaking his head. "I forgot the trap door for getting under the house is in here. I've never gone down it. Never needed to."

"It was open a little bit when I found it," Tyler said. "It looked like a good cat place. So I went down."

"That was brave of you," Dad said. "Good thing you had a flashlight." He looked hard at Tyler. "Did you find her?"

Tyler nodded.

"You found China?" Claire and I spoke at once.

"She likes it under the house," Tyler said. "We've been talking cat talk down there. She tells me what stuff to bring her."

We crowded around the trap door and peered into the darkness. When Tyler turned on the flashlight, we saw cobwebs and a gravelly floor. On the floor were cut-out paper fish and Legos and trucks. A bowl of water. A can of cat food.

Claire shuddered. "I bet there are bugs and spiders." She looked at Tyler in amazement.

"I see China," I said. "Hi, China." Far off in a back corner, two slitted eyes flashed. As Tyler moved the light, I could see metal heat ducts branching toward all parts of the house. No wonder China's voice had traveled through them.

"Hissssss!"

I jumped back into Dad's office.

"She's getting to be my friend," Tyler said. "I know how to talk to wild animals."

"You're some kid," Dad said. He brushed his hand across Tyler's red hair and then looked at his hand. "Cobwebs," he said.

Tyler shook his head and something black fell out of his ear. "She's all dirty too," he said. "She's lucky. She'll brush off." He looked up at Dad. "Am I in trouble?"

"You're a hero," Dad said. "A hero who needs a bath."

"We can help you tame her," I told Tyler. "We'll bring stuff to you. I've got a little ball with a jingle in it. And Claire made a thing out of beads that we can hang for her to hit with her paw." I looked down into the hole. "That *you* can hang," I said.

We ran to get stuff for China. Then, we did all the things that we'd written on the calendar. We sang songs. We read her poems and nursery rhymes. We bounced a ball. We brought more food.

China's slitted eyes never changed as she stared at us through the darkness of the crawl space.

Pretty soon we knew Tyler hadn't tamed her at all.

She was still wild.

Chapter 21

Tea with Ruby

Friday afternoon, Ruby phoned. "I'm home," she said.

"Did you read our note?" I asked when she let us in the door. "Did we do something wrong?"

"Harry Truman was old," Ruby said.

I looked closely at her. She looked sad. Did she blame us? I couldn't tell.

She was wearing silver tights. A silver cloth covered her curly hair and flowed down her back. She'd tied a purple scarf around her waist and little bells hung from the bottom of it and jingled as she moved. "Fish die," she said. "Anyone who has fish will tell you that."

"So, it wasn't our fault?" I asked. I had to be sure.

"Not your fault," she answered.

Claire heaved a sigh of relief.

Thick incense smells filled the room. Claire sneezed five times in the hallway. In Ruby's kitchen, Harry's plate lay on the counter.

We went to stand around him. "You made him beautiful," Ruby said. "Thank you." She held her hands over Harry's body and closed her eyes. "He's traveling a river," she said, "on his way to a different dream. I hear the water."

"Life is but a dream," Claire murmured. She looked up at Ruby, her eyes round with amazement.

"It's the kettle," I said. "Your water's boiling."

Ruby blinked her eyes and turned off the burner under the tea kettle. She took a blue-and-gold tin box out of the cupboard. "Will you stay for a cup of tea?" she asked.

As we nodded, Ruby dropped tea bags into mugs.

Claire moved closer to Ruby. "Before Harry died, I was going to ask my father if I could have some fish."

Ruby poured steaming water into the mugs and smells of roses and peppermint came out of the steam. "I hope you didn't change your mind," she said. "I love having fish. They're wonderful pets." We followed her to the dining room table and sat down.

"I'm never going to have a pet," Claire said. "You just get to like them, and then they die."

"I understand," Ruby said. "But if you never let yourself like something, you'll miss out on the fun of life. It's okay to love something that might die."

Claire shook her head. She stared into her mug. "My mother. . . ." Her voice trailed off. "I know you lost your mother," Ruby said. "But she loved you and you loved her. You have all your loving times to remember. Would you have told your mother you didn't want to love her, because she might die?"

"Of course not," Claire said.

Ruby bent toward her. "There are many things in this world for us to love. Friends and pets and everything around us." Her silver scarf fell

forward over her face and she pushed it back
with her hand. "We need to love them all as much
as possible." She picked up her tea and cradled
her hands around the mug. "If your dad says
it's okay to have fish, I can help you get started.
I've learned a lot about them over the last few
years."

Claire shifted her feet under the table. At
last, she looked up. "No," she said. "I mean, no,
thank you."

Ruby touched the back of Claire's hand. Then,
she turned to me. "Tell me how your business is
going," she said. "Did you have other pets to take
care of?"

I coughed on a swallow of tea. "Maybe we
should talk about something else," I said.

Ruby got the whole story out of us. She leaned
back in her chair. As she crossed her legs, bells
jingled at the edge of her skirt. "It sounds like
you girls did a good job. You worked hard."

"Do you think China Cat will get tame again?"
I asked.

"I don't know," Ruby answered.

"Could you maybe look it up?" Claire leaned forward. "Like in your crystal ball?"

Ruby laughed out loud. "I don't have a crystal ball," she said.

"Then how can you tell people's fortunes?" Claire asked.

Ruby smiled. "I use the Tarot cards," she said. "But all I do is lay out the cards. Each person does her own figuring out. If you girls come to visit me again, I can show you how the cards work."

After we finished our tea, Ruby paid us sixteen dollars. She said that was what she usually paid her regular pet sitter. We thanked her and started toward home.

"I like Ruby," Claire said. Rain sprinkled her hair with silver drops. She'd forgotten to open her umbrella.

"She's nice," I said.

"But still," Claire said, all at once snapping her umbrella open, "I'm not getting any fish. I don't care what she said. I'm not going to start liking something that's going to die."

Chapter 22

Two Moms

When we got home, Dad was in the kitchen, starting to make his famous toasted tuna sandwiches. "We have to talk about tomorrow," I told him.

"About Sierra getting back?" He stopped chopping the onion and laid down the big knife.

"What are we going to tell them?"

"The truth?" Dad asked.

I sighed. "That she's gone crazy? That she won't come out from under our house?"

Dad started again on the onions. Then he scraped the tiny pieces into the bowl of tuna salad. "Do you want olives?" he asked.

I nodded and got the olive jar from the refrigerator. "We didn't make her turn wild. She did it to herself as soon as she found out they were going to leave her here."

"I don't know what to do," Dad said. "Maybe we can offer them a new cat."

"They want China."

He nodded. "I know."

As he spread tuna on the bread slices, I thought about school on Monday and how Sierra wouldn't be speaking to me. Every recess, she'd play with someone else. We'd never play at each other's houses again. "Sadness makes me tired," I told Dad.

He stopped spreading tuna and held his arms out. Usually, Dad's hugs could take bad things away. But not this time.

That night when we got ready for bed, Claire was still talking about Ruby.

I pulled off my shoe and dropped it on the floor. Tomorrow, Claire would leave, and I'd get my room back. If it weren't for China, by Sunday everything would be back to normal.

"Want to see my mother?" Claire asked.

I stared at her.

She reached under her pillow and pulled out that pencil case. She opened it, took out a photograph, and turned it toward me. In the photo, a woman was sitting on the steps of Claire's front porch. Her blonde hair shone in the sunlight. She was holding a little girl.

"Is that you?" I asked. "On her lap?"

Claire nodded.

I studied the face of the woman in the picture and looked again at Claire. "You look just like her," I said.

Claire stared at me. Then she smiled. "That's the nicest thing you ever said to me, Katie."

I handed back the photo. "It's true."

"Can I see your mom?" Claire asked.

I paused, one sock on, one off. I could almost feel Mom's poster, right under me, under my bed. But what if Claire said something mean about Mom?

I reached under my bed. Touched the rolled-up poster.

I pulled it out a little bit. Then, I pushed it back. "You won't like her."

"Why?" Claire asked.

"Because she's still alive."

"You *are* lucky. Your mother's only gone to another state." Claire jumped down beside me on the floor. She sat close to me, in her blue-and-white striped pajamas. "Show me, anyway."

"I'm not lucky," I said. "This is worse."

Claire shook her head. "Nothing's worse than dying."

"My mother could be here," I said slowly, "but she doesn't want to be."

Claire was silent, her blue eyes looking back at me. All at once, her eyes filled with tears.

I swallowed. "I don't know why she likes singing so much," I said, blinking back my tears. "She likes singing more than being my mom."

There. I'd said it. Something I'd been thinking for a long time. I kicked at the foot of my bed. Ouch! I hunched over and rubbed my toe.

Claire hugged her knees to her chest. "I guess my mom liked going skiing. She could have stayed home with me that day." She rubbed her tears away with her pajama sleeve. "If only I'd been sick. But how could I know which day was the one for getting sick?" She sighed. "We both lost our moms," she said. "And both our moms made us mad. And sad."

Both our moms. . . .

I reached again under the bed. This time, I pulled out the poster and unrolled it. I stared at Mom's smile. I was still scared. What would Claire say?

"Wow!" Claire said. "Cute clothes."

Giggles snorted out my nose. I should have known. Of course, Claire would love my mom's sparkly vest.

Chapter 23

The Final Tail

By Saturday afternoon, my room looked like me again. Mom's poster hung next to my dresser. Claire had rolled up her pale blue rug and filled her bags with her blue stationery, her projects, and her clothes. Her mother's photo stood on the bedside table. She was writing in her notebook. Her face looked somehow softer; she was even smiling.

"Pen pals?" I asked.

She looked up and shook her head. "A list. I like those yellow-and-black striped ones, and I want those blue ones with the black eye things. And one of those flat ones. . . ."

"You're getting fish?"

She nodded. "I think we ARE supposed to love things," she said, "even if they might die."

Ruby's words. That made sense to me, too.

I looked at Claire. Had she changed? Or was I just getting used to her? "Thanks for being my business partner," I said.

She hugged the notebook against her chest. "Thanks for letting me."

The doorbell rang.

Claire started toward the door. "I hope it's my father. I hope it's not Sierra."

We heard Dad open the front door. "How was Hawaii?" he asked.

Claire and I froze.

"Sunshine the whole time," Sierra's mom answered. "Look at my tan."

"I got a tan, too," Sierra's voice said.

"Rained here almost every day," Dad said.

I touched Claire's arm. "We have to get this over with."

In the hallway, we almost bumped into Tyler. "Come on, China," he said. "Come see who's here."

"Mew," China Cat said.

Claire and I stopped short. We stared at China.

"Mew," she said again. She waved her tail at us. She wound herself around Tyler's legs and pushed her head up for a pat as she passed in front of him.

"Nice kitty," Tyler crooned.

China walked down the hall beside Tyler. Her hips swayed. She sang a deep, happy song. "There you are," Mrs. Dymond said. "Why, you look great, China!"

I heard Dad drop something on the floor. "Huh?" he asked.

Claire and I went to stand in the front hall as China bounded into Mrs. Dymond's arms and nuzzled her head under her chin.

Sierra grinned at me and handed me a box. "I brought a pretty shell for your collection," she said. But then, her grin faded as she looked behind me. At Claire.

"I was at Katie's house all week," Claire said. "We're business partners now."

Sierra's mouth dropped open.

"That reminds me," Mrs. Dymond said. "We owe Katie forty dollars." She passed China to Mr. Dymond and got out her checkbook.

I went to stand beside her. "Wait," I said.

"I suppose you'll split it with Claire," Mrs. Dymond said, "since she's your business partner." She began to write the check.

"No," I said. "I mean, yes. But mostly, it's Tyler's."

Beside me, Claire nodded. Dad cleared his throat and nodded, too.

Tyler shoved his hands into his pockets. All at once, he looked five instead of four. "China liked me the best," he said proudly.

"I'll write the check to Katie," Mrs. Dymond said, "and the three of you can decide how to split it."

While Claire and Tyler collected cat toys, Sierra and I carried some of China's stuff out to her car. "Lots to tell you," I told her as we shoved things into the back seat.

"Poor you," Sierra said. "Claire was at your house all week?"

"It was an awful week," I answered, "but not because of Claire."

"What could be worse than Claire?" Sierra rolled her eyes.

I tipped my face up and tasted rain on my tongue. "A bunch of things are worse," I said.

As Claire came up to us with a bag filled with paper fish and jingly toys, I began a list: "Piddle puddles. Green vomit. Monster cat. Yes, Sierra, your cat went crazy."

"But Tyler did too," Claire said. "And Harry Truman died. . . ."

Sierra put her hands over her ears. "Next year," she said, "you guys have to get out of Oregon."

I thought about vacations coming up. People going on trips. Pets left lonely and sad with no one to take care of them. Now that I thought back, the week hadn't been *that* bad.

"Maybe I'll stick around," I said. "A lonely pet might need me."

Anne Warren Smith grew up in the Adirondack Mountains of upstate New York. She now lives in Corvallis, Oregon, where she has shared the house with three dogs—Taco and Lucy, plus Muffin, who is the dog in this story. When not working on a new book, she teaches creative writing, walks the Oregon beaches, and noodles on her harp.

Katie Jordan's story began with *Turkey Monster Thanksgiving*. Watch for *Bittersweet Summer*, the third book in the series, coming soon!

More information about the author is at www.annewarrensmith.com.

Turkey Monster
Thanksgiving

Anne Warren Smith

Read all three stories
about Katie Jordan!

Turn the page
for a sneak peek at
Bittersweet Summer

Tails of
Spring Break

Anne Warren Smith

Bittersweet
Summer

Anne Warren Smith

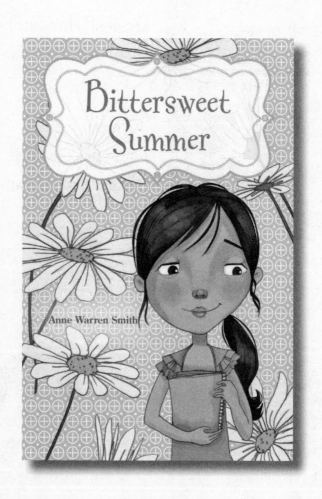

Chapter 1

The Last Day of Fourth Grade

The Fourth Grade room was unusually quiet as the line of sad kids shuffled forward. We were saying good-bye to Ms. Morgan.

I swallowed back my tears and tasted end-of-school fruit punch and end-of-school lemon cupcakes. My throat hurt and my stomach gurgled as I got into the good-bye line.

Claire Plummer stepped in next to me. "She's

the most beautiful teacher I ever had," she said in a dreary, woeful voice as she tugged at her blond curls. Claire hoped that tugging would make her hair longer, but she would never have a long, beautiful ponytail like Ms. Morgan's. Besides, Ms. Morgan's hair was brown.

"Fifth grade will be fun," Ms. Morgan said to Tiffany who was four people ahead of us. "You'll see."

"I already hate fifth grade," I said to my best friend, Sierra, who stood on the other side of me. She and Claire nodded. We all sighed.

Ms. Morgan hugged Doug Backer and then Ethan Murphy and then Alex Ramirez.

"How can she stand hugging Alex in that old, ratty shirt?" Claire whispered.

"It doesn't smell," Sierra said. All at once, her face turned red. "He sat in front of me," she added. "I sniffed it once."

We giggled.

Maybe, I thought, Alex loved that flannel shirt the way I loved my orange hooded sweatshirt.

Of course, my sweatshirt didn't hang down to my knees. And I didn't wear it to school every day.

"Hi, Claire," Ms. Morgan said as Claire stepped forward. "You and your dad made this a special year for me."

"It was our pleasure," Claire's dad called from the back of the room. He had been the room father all year. Now, he was doing his last chores: gathering up paper napkins and paper cups from the party. He had made the lemon cupcakes. I swallowed again as Ms. Morgan hugged Claire.

Claire had been the perfect student. I had not. Three times, I had over-watered the sunflower. Three times, muddy water had flooded the windowsills.

Sierra got the next hug. "I loved seeing your rock collection," Ms. Morgan said to her. "You might grow up to be a scientist."

"Thanks for being my teacher," Sierra said.

As I stepped forward, I wondered if Ms. Morgan was secretly glad I was going on to fifth grade. I had done so many terrible things.

When I added extra lines to my part in the class play, everybody forgot what they were supposed to do next. When I bumped into the big shamrock poster on St. Patrick's Day, it knocked everything off Ms. Morgan's desk. Her purse, three jars of pencils, a box of filing cards, her big dictionary.

"Good-bye," I said and started to leave. But she took both my hands and pulled me close.

"Katie," she said. "You were my most . . ." She stopped to think. ". . .my most enthusiastic student."

"Thanks," I mumbled.

"You get excited about things. That's a wonderful way to be." She smiled her beautiful smile, and her green eyes sparkled. "I bet you will have adventures this summer."

"I might," I answered, happy that she was acting like she really liked me. I breathed deep to keep her vanilla-pudding smell with me as long as possible.

Sierra tugged on my arm. "My mom is probably waiting," she said.

I ran to gather up my artwork. We couldn't put it off any longer.

Fourth grade was over, and my summer adventures were about to begin.